Fun With Hats

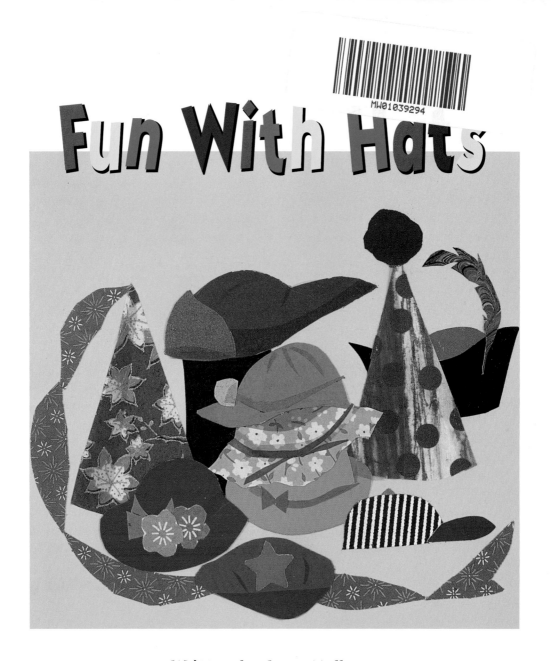

Written by Lucy Malka
Illustrated by Melinda Levine

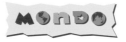

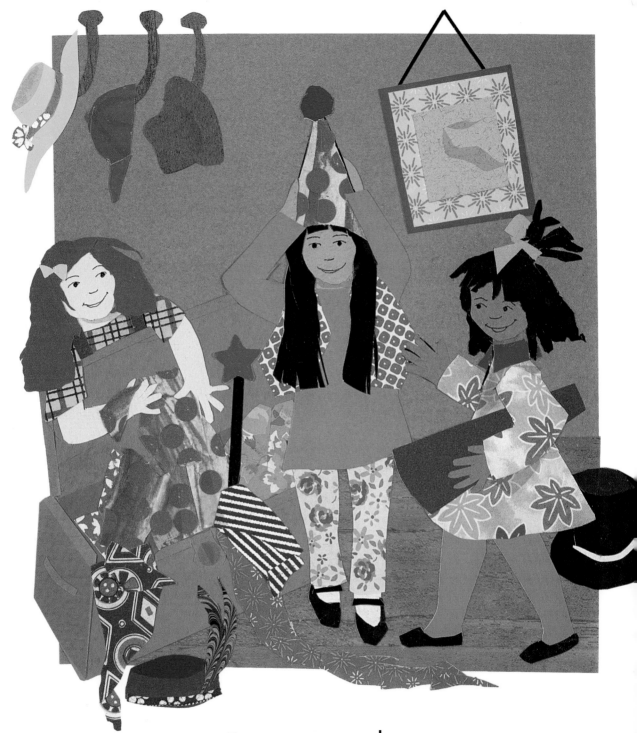

I put on a hat.

Now I am a clown.

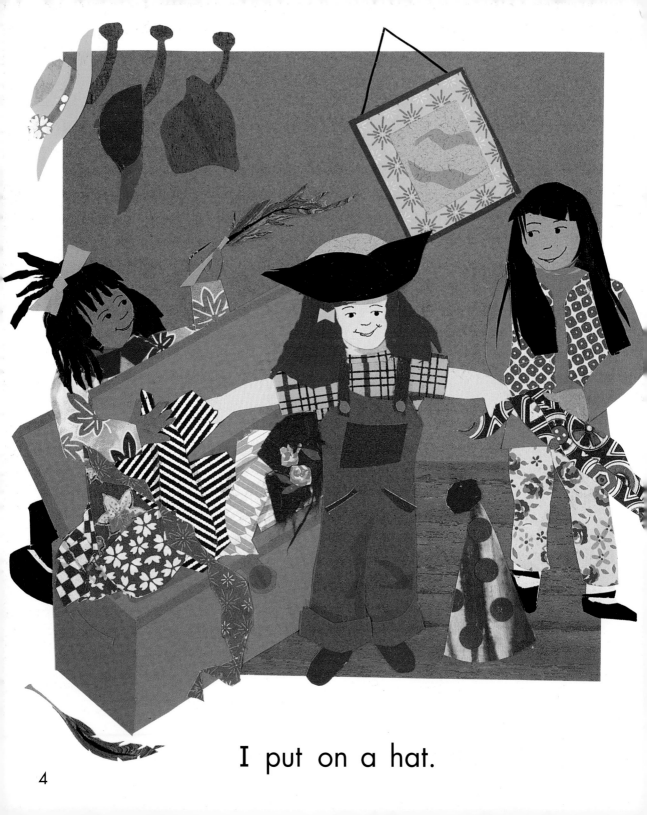

I put on a hat.

4

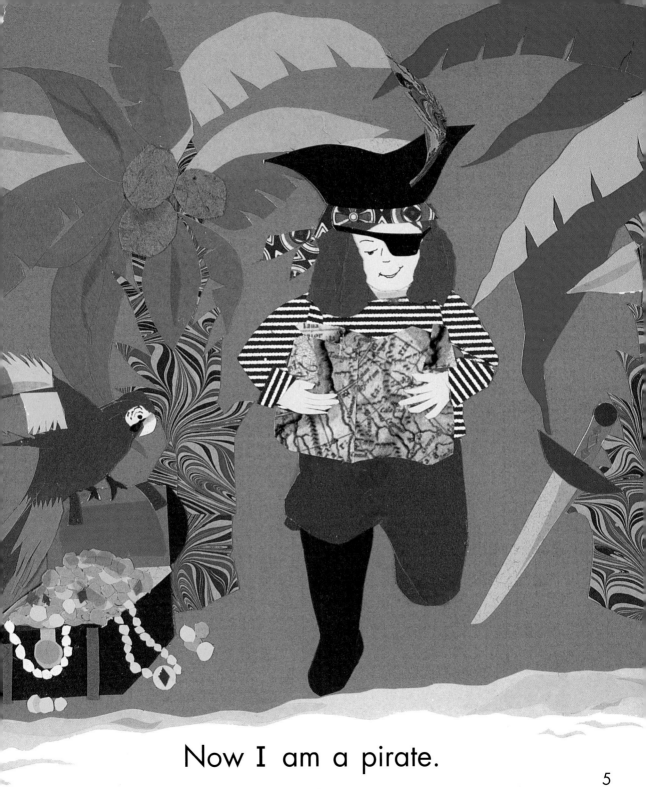

Now I am a pirate.

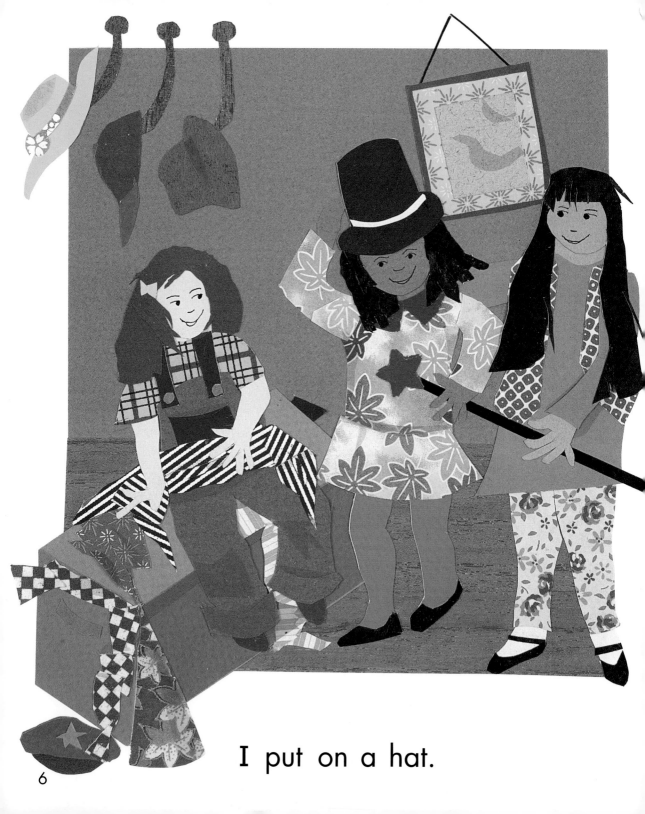

I put on a hat.

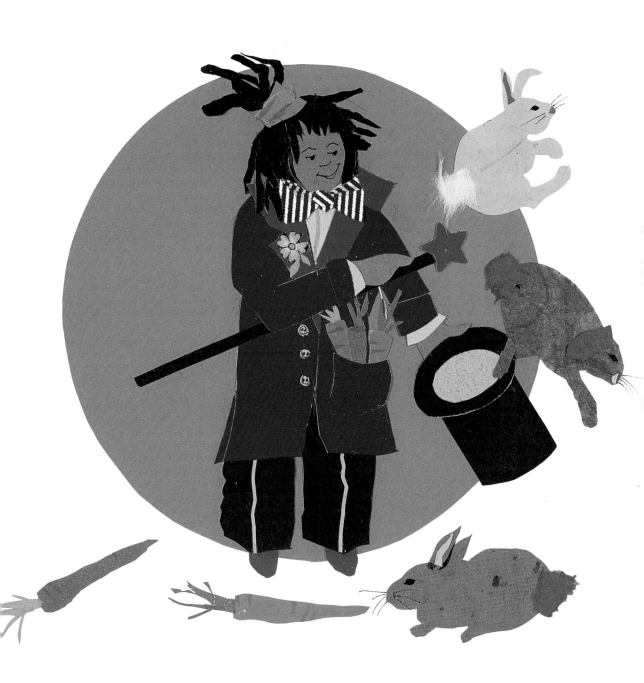

Now I am a magician.

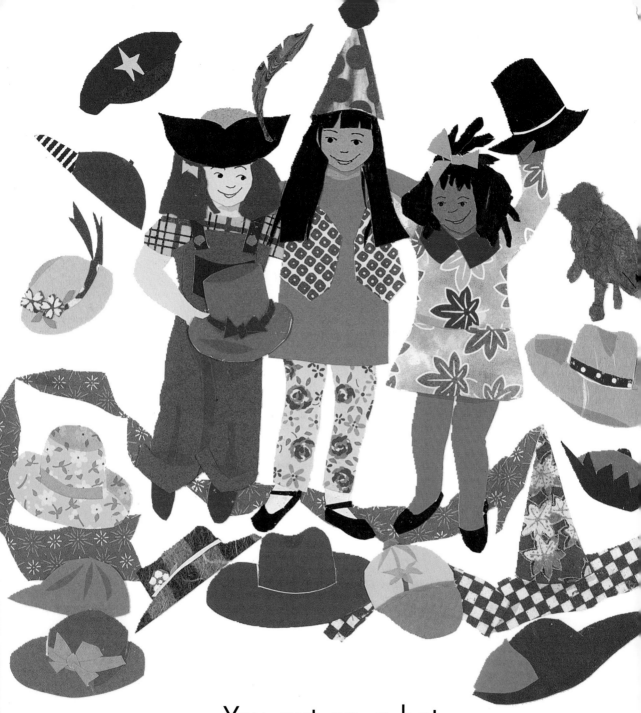

You put on a hat.
What are you?